The Clock Strikes One

Z. Pyke

DEDICATION

I dedicate this book to my wonderful daughter. Thank you for always making me strive to give my absolute best and for being my saving grace. I wouldn't be able to do all this without you.
Love Mum

ACKNOWLEDGMENTS

Thank you to every single person who reads this book!

Always know you are wonderful and you matter.

1

It all began when I was merely five years old, a time when destiny was scripted for me. I was foretold about the trajectory of my life, the inevitable inheritance of the role of the town's finest detective from none other than my father—Detective Montrose. A man whose record boasted a flawless 100% case closure rate. As the town echoed with claims that I was destined to carry on his legacy, I couldn't shake the feeling that I would forever dwell in his imposing shadow. Still, fueled by determination, I yearned to surpass him at his own game.

Miles or Detective Kane as he proudly reminds people, is my right hand man. We have been best friends since I started at the academy and he has slotted into life with Lucy and I perfectly, I couldn't ask for two better friends to support me.

Our town is small and rural, Miles and I are the only detectives for miles. The trees that hug the area make for an eerie feel once fog rolls in and the sun hides. We barely get much trouble, it's normally pretty easy going. The town is held together by the farms that surround it, it's lucky we have them as the nearest city is about four hours away.

****

"Have you heard from Lucy?" I asked Miles.

"Not for about 3 days, you know how she gets when she is having one of her episodes, i'm sure we will hear from her soon" he reassured.

"Yeah but i went around to her place, the blinds are up and she isn't there but her car and phone are"

Miles reassured me that I was just being a paranoid detective and she had probably gone for a run.
She did this often when she was "manic" she would lock herself away and hide from absolutely everyone. One time Miles and I found her, passed out in the middle of the street after taking some random pills she got from the teenagers at the skatepark. Miles stayed with her, got her well and sober while I worked to pay everyone's bills. We became a family. I knew Lucy and I knew something wasn't right.
I finished work at 6:00pm and headed around to Lucy's to see if she had come back. I got to her door, knocked, tried the handle and it opened the door. Not unusual for Lucy or anyone in this town to leave things unlocked.
The living room was tidy, her phone sitting on the coffee table.

"Luce are you home?!" I yelled.

I got no reply, just a deafening silence. I walked down the hall, past the bathroom and the laundry and made my way upstairs to her bedroom. I opened the door to a perfectly clean room, the bed unslept in, the window wide open. Again, it was strange but not out of the ordinary around here. I locked the house up and headed home but I couldn't sleep, my mind in a constant state of detective mode as I tried to think of anything that may have been out of the ordinary for Lucy to leave without taking anything. Especially her phone.

5:00am came around and it was time to drag myself out of bed and to the coffee shop before work. I couldn't handle one of Miles's chats on why coffee melts your brain so I wasn't going to be making one at work. Plus, I need a double shot of something.
I got to work before anyone else. I work with great people but they could put you straight to sleep with some of the stories they tell. Being early meant I had time to enjoy my coffee and open some emails that I had been putting off.

"Clara! my one and only prodigy" A detective exclaimed.

I sighed a heavy sigh *"Goodmorning Detective Montrose, or better yet, EX Detective. Have you come to stock up the snack fridge? Replenish the towels in the shower rooms?"*

"Oh come on, not even a Hey Dad, what are you up to?" he replied

I rolled my eyes and chose to ignore him. My dad and I didn't always see eye to eye, he was a great detective but a lousy father. When mum died, he lost his touch and after the incident a few years back, he also lost his job, his purpose.I was amidst my thoughts when the ringing of my phone startled me

"Hello, this is Detective Montrose, what can I help you with today?"

Soft whimpering of a female

"Hello, was anyone there? ma'am i'm going to need you to stop crying so i can help you okay?"

gasp
"Clar…Clara. Its…Lu..Lucy"
whimpering

"Lucy? What the hell, where are you? Why are you crying?'

Lucy's voice dropped to a whisper *"I need your help. I've been, I've been taken. I don't know where i am "*

Lucy starts to softly cry

"and I think they're going to kill me. No..no..no they're coming"

"Lucy what do you mean? Where are you?" "LUCY" I yelled.

Then the line went dead.

2

My blood ran cold as I tried processing what I had just heard on the phone. It can't be right, it has to be some elaborate prank. Right? It has to be. It can't be true. Not Lucy, not my Lucy.
I was trying to contain my emotions to not let anyone else ask what had happened. Then I received a text from the same number Lucy had called on.

"Till the clock strikes one"

Then once again nothing, I tried to call but the phone was now off. I couldn't wrap my head around what was happening but I needed to find out soon.
Miles got to work at 9am and I ushered him into one of the meeting rooms, I had to tell him before anyone else.

I explained what had happened but he didn't believe me at first and honestly, I didn't even believe myself. I was still holding it together but the reality began to sink in when Miles asked;

"What if it is real? What if she really needs our help Clara?"

And he was right, we needed to take it seriously and figure out what was going on. I walked back to my desk, Miles sat down beside me and we started to gather all information and events leading to when we last heard from Lucy.

Miles hadn't seen her since Monday, 4 days ago and he said that she had come across absolutely fine but she had been nervously checking her phone the whole time he was with her. He had seen her the day before and she was barely even looking at her phone to check the time. So it was certainly odd.

"We should probably go around to her place again, I have her spare key" I offered.

Miles agreed, we finished out our work day by 2pm and both headed over to Lucy's. We didn't need a key, the door was wide open and the place was an absolute mess, like someone was looking for something, not trying to destroy something.

We looked around searching for any sign of Lucy but found nothing.

"I.. was here yesterday, the place was spotless" I explained

"I don't understand why anyone would do this to her," Miles replied.

"I know but we also know, this wouldn't be the first instance of her being in with the wrong crowd" I sighed.

Then my phone rang. My body went cold as I recognised the number.

Lucy.

"Clara. Clara, can you hear me? I don't have much time till they come back. The clock strikes one. You need to remember Clara. I need you to remember." She whispered.

****beep* *beep* *beep****

The line went dead. I didn't even have a chance to respond. Miles and I looked at each other, stunned and confused. While I tried to think of what she meant by the clock strikes one, it was evident that we needed to work fast and quickly to find her.

By 9:00pm, Miles decided to head home and get some sleep while I stayed at Lucy's. I was going through everything I could to try and find something that would link to her saying "the clock strikes one". I couldn't figure out why that was so important.

I didn't want to, but I needed my dad, he was a fresh pair of eyes and I needed the help plus he would love the ego boost of me asking for it.

Dad got around to Lucy's at about 11:00 pm. I got him caught up and his face went white. Lucy was family, I had grown up with her. To me she was a sister, to dad, a daughter. He leant on the kitchen bench and sighed.

"We can't let them get away with this. We have to find her. After her sister… I… I can't let her down again Clara, i can't" he started to cry as the memories flooded his mind.

****

Jason Montrose was Australia's best detective and raising his daughter to do exactly what he did made everyone adore him. 2019 was a busy year , with COVID and lockdowns, things were tough, my dad thought he had it bad. Towards the end of the year however, he got a case early one morning. A young girl, only 18, had been reported missing. It was Lucy's little sister Marley who was 10 years younger than Lucy. Lucy had practically raised her. Dad was the lead detective, searching all over for her. In the end her body was discovered in the nearby lake, she was mutilated beyond imagination, dental being the only way we knew it was her. A few months later, the guy who they suspected did it hung himself in his home. He lived next door to the girls. There was no sign it was ever him, they had no idea. My dad retired not long after that. He couldn't handle feeling like he had let everyone down, Lucy especially. Lucy didn't take it well. She barely survived it if i'm honest.

3

Dad and I began turning Lucy's house upside down just trying to find anything we could to make a link to where she might be. I was in her room, pacing, waiting for something to come into my mind. Studying the pictures of us on the walls like I was expecting them to talk. Looking at the one pink wall in a natural coloured room made me laugh, she was always the spontaneous one out of us.

Then I remembered she had a little keepsake box in her wardrobe, if there was anything she wanted hidden for me to find, it would be in there.

I got the box and placed it on the bed, peeling the lid off it revealed a musky smell of cigarette and wine. Within the box I found some old photos, we looked about 10 or 11. So young and clueless of what life had in store for us. In the background of one photo was my family cabin. It was out past the town and further into the forest. Honestly like something out of a creepy horror movie but we loved going out there when dad was away in the city. It made us feel as if it was just us two against the world when we would go there. Even as teens there was something so magical about the serenity out there.

I walked downstairs to find Miles had arrived and joined dad with searching the house. Suddenly another call came through, this time from a different number.

"Hello, is this Clara? We know where Lucy is. We can help you find her" the voice was that of a scared female

"What?! How do you know? Who are you?"

"We just know"

"HOW?!" i yelled, trying to hide my panic

"Because we were paid to kidnap her"

My breath quickened and my knees went weak *"wh…wh..what?"*

"Look, you can't go to this about anyone else. Do not trust the local police. We know where you are, we will come to you" A male answered before the line went dead.

I felt my stomach drop and all the colour drain from my face. Miles and dad looked mortified. Why couldn't we trust the people we had always worked with, some we even went into the academy with. It didn't make any sense.

About 20 minutes later a male and female walked in the back door. My dad was the first to make any move and scruffed the male by his shirt.

"What the HELL do you know?!" he growled through gritted teeth.

"Please don't hurt him! We will tell you everything we know. I am Jess and that's Leon" she points to Leon who is absolutely terrified.

Jess

Leon and I have been together for what feels like our whole lives. We were drop outs, castaways, kids our parents didn't want. So we borrowed a bit of money that we couldn't pay back. We thought we could run away and all our problems would be gone and for the most part they were. But then we started getting followed by strange cars that shouldn't be out this far. We knew that our "loans" were starting to catch up to us and we couldn't run away this time.

So when we got a call, offering us a way out with no questions asked. We said yes. Then another call came in to say we needed to kidnap a girl and take her to the furthest farm west, for $100,000. We said yes.

We have no idea who the guy was but he seemed so calm, like this wasn't the first time he had done it. The police badge he kept on his waist told us not to question him though,

We waited till the girl was asleep before sneaking into her house, dragging her and throwing her in the boot of our car and then we were told to trash the place and take any files we found. The request was to make it look like a kidnapping or something. She just kept screaming for a girl named Clara, once she woke up. We drove to the far west of town before turning down a dirt road to a farm, surrounded by the horrible trees that plagued the town. When we arrived the house looked like it wasnt even lived in but our instructions were to throw the girl into the large blue shipping container, lock it up, leave any files and drive away.

"Leon, something didn't feel right about that…. She had just lost a baby"

"You're just getting in your own head. He probably just made up a story so we wouldn't ask questions" he replied.

The $100,000 was in our account 2 hours later. But I bet, if we get ahold of Clara, we could score even more money to tell her where we dropped the girl and after a quick google and finding her to be some hot shot detective. We knew we'd get our money

****

"Take us there NOW!" I snapped.

Jess looked more collected than Leon but she shook her head profusely.

"Calm down, you need to head West all the way past the end of town, then turn right down the dirt road and follow it till you get to an old farmhouse. She's in a blue shipping container. Well she was. When we left. BUT we want more money or we will tell the

guy that you are onto him and you'll never find her" explained Jess

Dad dropped Leon and he fell to the floor. ***"Fine an extra $50,000. Nothing more"*** Dad huffed.

They both nodded their heads. Miles and I went looking for this apparent farm and dad stayed with them to sort out the money.

4

Miles and I headed west, as far as the road would take us and as fast as he could. I could barely process what they had told me. How did I miss that? I should have been there. I pushed the thoughts aside, I was determined to find out the truth. I was going to make up for my mistake.

"I think that's the road to the right," said Miles

It snapped me out of my guilty trance and I nodded at him. We turned onto a bumpy, barely visible dirt road. The dense trees and lingering winter fog made for an eerie trip into the unknown. The road felt like it went on forever as we passed burnt cars, fallen trees, and small wallabies. I glanced at Miles, who was taking in the creepy scenery that surrounded us. My heart raced with anticipation, as we continued. I couldn't help but feel a sense of dread creep over me, I knew we were in a hateful place.
Our gazes were drawn to a clearing surrounded by trees, where we

spotted a farmhouse that seemed uninhabited. Almost as if it had been here for centuries. Then I saw it, the rusted blue shipping container. We were at the right place.

I shot out of the car barely remembering to take off my seatbelt and sprinted for the container. There was a chain wrapped around the bars to open it but the padlock holding the chains was unlocked. I frantically removed them and Miles helped to pry open the container.

"We're here Lucy! We're here!" I cried

The door squealed open to reveal nothing. Not a single damn thing inside. I stood there, confused. I could feel my heart pounding in my chest as the reality of the situation sank in. We had come all this way for nothing. I slowly walked away, feeling a sense of disappointment and defeat wash over me. We had spent so much time, effort, and money to get here, and it had all been for nothing. Time was running out to find her. I needed to look for the next lead. I couldn't give up, I had to keep going. We had to find her, no matter what.

"No, no, no, no. This can't be happening. Miles what the hell is happening" My emotions took over as i started to cry. Lucy was gone.

"We will find her, Clara. We can't give up, let's look around" Miles calmly replied.

The sound of a car tearing up the gravel behind us startled me. I spun to see my dad, he could see the empty container, and his face was expressionless. He came up and held me as we both cried, wondering where we went wrong. How could the best of the best miss this?

We agreed to split up and search around to make sure nothing was missed. Or maybe she had gotten out and escaped somehow.

Dad checked around and inside the container, Miles searched the perimeter near the trees and I took the farmhouse. The steps creaked behind me as I walked up them. Almost like they were about to snap in half.
I searched high and low for something that might lead me to Lucy but all I found was dust and spiders. I walked out of the house looking around the outside, when something caught my eye sitting in a wet muddy puddle. I walked over to pick it up, it was a business card.

'Head of Police

Harry Cornmad

0408125633'

"MILES!" I yelled. ***"You need to see this, right now"***

Miles came running over and so did Dad. ***"What is it?"*** Miles asked

My dad snatched the card out of my hand. With a concerned look he said, ***"there's no way. This can't be right."***

I couldn't believe it either. Harry was my dad's age, Lucy and I had grown up around him. But if he is in on this, where the hell is Lucy? And what did he want with her?

5

I felt defeated and burnt out. After three days without much sleep, I was determined not to rest until I found her. We had run out of possibilities, had no leads, no trace, and no other place to turn for assistance. Harry might be working with someone else on this. We had to prevent him from catching on. Miles and I made the decision to go to my family's cabin to see if we could magically remember something there.
A little after midday, we arrived at the cabin. With the fog being persistent, it sent a chill down my spine that almost made me gasp. I couldn't force myself to get out of the car and just sat there. I snapped out of my daze as Miles placed his hand on my arm.

His hand felt sweaty on my skin, and his voice went raspy. ***"Clara, you can't hold yourself responsible.. We'll find her,"*** he promised.

However, I did hold myself responsible. I was the one who should have protected her and so I placed more blame on myself than on anyone else. God, I can't even begin to comprehend how terrified she would be.

Tears started to stream down my cheeks as I felt my lips tremble. Miles's hold on my arm became tighter.

"Clara. Don't do this. Don't fall apart on me, i need you in this"

"I know. Miles I couldn't do this without…"

I was interrupted by my phone ringing, *"you can answer it, it'll be dad, just tell him we are looking for new leads"* i said to Miles as Iwiped away my tears.

"Clara. It's the number…. That, that, Lucy called on" he stumbled.

I grabbed the phone and answered *"Lucy, where are you?"* I panicked not knowing when the call would cut out again.

"Clara.. You need to save him.. It's too late for me.. Save him Clara" Lucy began to cry as she screamed *"SAVE HIM!"*

Then the line, for a third time, went dead. Miles and I were frozen, looking at each other in disbelief.

"W…What does she mean 'save him'" Miles finally asked.

"I'm not sure. She sounded so afraid, Miles. How in the hell are we going to handle this?"

We were still sitting in the car, the windows were fogged and the air thick and hot. I needed a moment. I got out of the car and looked back at Miles. His head was in his hands and I had realized he had not yet really had any emotion to all of this. He felt bad but he was staying neutral, positive. I quickly realized I would be an absolute mess without him keeping his composure. I started walking towards the cabin when I noticed large tyre tracks that definitely didn't come from Miles's tiny car.
I didn't want to call dad, he was so exhausted and upset, he needed the rest but I'm pretty sure he said he hadn't been out here in months, so they're unlikely to have come from him.
The rain we've had has turned the ground into a thick mud and I could see the tires were leading to, deeper into the thick bushland.

"Miles, come here!"

Miles jumped out of the car and ran over to me ***"Shit, could that be something?"*** he said

"I believe so"

"Let's go then" Miles started to follow the tracks and I made my way behind him.

The searching would be on foot from here, Miles's car would never make it. Rushing through the tall grass following these tracks gave me hope again. The fog was still rolling in, making the view in front of us barely visible. We had to rely on the tracks and not fear where they were going. My mind kept racing over what Lucy could possibly mean by telling me I had to save him but maybe someone else was with her, maybe they were both keeping each other alive and sane. I wondered if it could even mean that Harry would come for Miles next but I didn't dare to voice these speculations to Miles.

****bzzz* *bzzz****

I got a text from dad;

"Hi Clara. Haven't found anything around Harry's desk or his police car. What about you guys?"

I wanted to tell him that I had heard from Lucy but he had been so stressed, I just couldn't, not until we had some idea of where these tracks went. Hopefully they lead to something.

6

Looking for any signs of Lucy for what felt like hours, we kept following the tracks. But all I found was knee high grass and more trees. Then the tracks just stopped, another dead end in this runaround. The grass was thick and you could easily tell that there were no longer any tracks.

I felt my heart thumping in my chest while the birds chirped above us. You could get lost in the serenity out here, the air smelt and even felt so pure and fresh. It made me think of how often Lucy and I would go exploring out past the cabin, never this far out but far enough for it to seem like we were the only two people on earth. She would always go on about how lucky we were to be "sisters by choice" and in a way that somehow made us feel like superheroes.

"I can't believe they didn't go anywhere" I huffed.

"Least we followed them and we know now that nothing is here" Miles replied

"I can't keep up with this wild goose chase, Miles"

Miles walked off, mumbling something under his breath. It was cold and foggy and both of us were exhausted but we needed to stay focused. I had to keep my mind on what we were trying to do and that was to find Lucy, no matter what.

"CLARA! You need to see this" Miles shouted

I ran over to him as quickly as I could. When I got to him, I could only just see his head within the long grass as he kneeled in the mud. My heart was racing and my body felt heavy.

"What the hell… is that?" I Asked

Miles was nealed looking into a deep, dark and dirty hole. It looked almost abandoned.
The town was built many years ago to support miners but we were always told that all of the mine shafts were closed off or they had filled them in so no one wandered off and fell in one. But yet, here we were, in the area the tracks stopped looking deep into what we suspect is none other than a mine shaft.

Miles yelled into the hole ***"Hello! Hello?"***

"This has to be one of the old mine shafts" I knelt down beside him.

"I think so but why hasn't this one been filled in?" he asked.

We both decided we needed a way down to have a look and rule the possibility of Lucy falling in and not being able to get out. I looked at my phone and noticed that I had some cell reception here. I had to call dad.

ring*ring*ring

"Clara? What's going on?"

"Look I Didn't want to say anything if we didn't have a lead but at the cabin, Miles and I found some tire tracks. We followed them about an hour west, on foot and Dad, we found a mine shaft out here"

"That's impossible. They were all closed up. You said West right?"

"Yeah, from the cabin"

"Shit. Clara, i'm on my way right now, i'll bring what I can to get down there"

"Dad, you sound worried, what's going on?"

"That land, is Downsen Land"

We both went quiet and then I realized what that meant. Dads voice interrupted my thoughts as he said

"Clara, that land belongs to Harry's family"

end call

I felt sick. Like I had just been punched in the stomach, then the panic started to set in that maybe Lucy wasn't okay at all. Miles's face dropped as I explained to him what dad had just said. It was the first time I saw him look even slightly stressed about the situation. Time stood still while we waited for dad to come. He pulled up and ran out with a rope and harness.

Looks like one of us is heading down into that mine shaft after all. I got secured into the harness, Dad and Miles then began to lower me down the hole. It was dark, creepy and it just felt evil descending down there. I touched the ground with a sigh of relief as I coughed from the thick dust that lingered in the air.

"Guys, I think I can see some light down this pathway, you need to get down here"

7

Eventually, Miles and Dad found their way into the hole. With the only light coming from the right, we took a look around. We started walking down the route once I turned on my phone's torch. We reached a gap in the path to the left. It was obvious that someone had been here recently even before you walked in. Miles stooped to feel the footprints left by their shoes in the clay and dirt.

"These aren't that old, maybe a day or a few hours" he said

"Let's have a look around then" I exhaled loudly

It was hard pushing through emotion and exhaustion. No one had really slept and we didn't have all the resources we normally would. This could well and truly be another deadend.

I walked over to the middle of the room, it was dark and musky but there were lights and hopefully there was power. After looking around, we found a breaker box in the back corner, and when switching the power on, lights around us and along the path began to flicker and come alive. They revealed a space that felt like a villain's lair.

I walked back over to the desk, which was neatly organized. From left to right, there was a pencil, a notebook and a coffee cup. Definitely not something left years and years ago when this place was up and running. I began to turn pages of the notebook, the majority of them had been ripped out. In the back however was one lonely page. Not completely ripped out, the leftover paper read;

"I need to find those files. The footage. Everything. I think they're starting to suspect something"

I walked the notebook over to my dad, he studied the pages and took one large gulp as his throat went dry.

"Clar, I know that handwriting and neatness… It all makes sense. Its Harry"

"It can't be, surely. He's older, how would he even get down here?"

"I don't know but it's definitely his writing"

Miles yelled out *"Guys we should probably keep going, see if we can find a way out before it gets dark or he comes back"*

We continued back on the path. Still coughing and squinting at the thick dust that surrounded us and rose every step we took. I could see ahead that there was another clearing, this time infront of us, stopping the path. Miles had frozen in his tracks, barely moving, heck he was hardly breathing. I went to push past him but he stopped me, placing his arm out to try and force me back.

His voice dropped and cracked, *" Clara dont. Just wait here"*

He slowly walked off, dragging his feet almost as if he was a small child that didn't want to leave the toy shop. I moved forward, my dad right behind me and we stood at the door scouting the area. My hand covered my mouth almost against my will as I felt my dad place a tight grip on my shoulder.

The room was bigger than the last but the path had ended and it was just a big open room. Along the left side were three beds separated by three walls.. The third bed I couldn't really see from where we were standing but the other two I could.
There were handcuffs tied to the tops of the two beds I could see, and dried blood had discolored the mattresses. Miles was walking around the second bed when my intuition told me I needed to see the third one, it was like something was pulling me to it.
My dad started to investigate the first bed and I headed for the third.
I made my way down to the bed, I didn't need to walk very far before I saw it. Saw her. It felt like my heart had been ripped out, I forgot how to breathe, how to speak.

"No… No…. No no no no no. NO!" I screamed till there was no air left in my lungs. I rushed over to Lucy, her lifeless hands still chained to the bed frame. I grabbed my cuff keys and got her

wrists free. I clung to her desperately, tears streaming down my face. Denial gripped my heart as I struggled to accept the harsh reality. Cradling her lifeless form on my lap, I gently brushed the strands of hair away from her still face, clutching onto her, unable to let go.

"I'm so sorry Lucy! I am so sorry"

Miles came running over. He stopped at the bed and walked away, he was never good at showing his emotions. Then dad walked over, slowly, he wasn't stupid, he knew, he knew what was going to be there. Without saying a thing, he sat next to me and held me, while we sat rocking. I had utterly lost myself at that moment. After years of doing this job, you become attuned to the strong difference between life and death. She had been gone for a considerable time, and I arrived too late to save her from this terrifying end.

"Come on Clar. Lets get her some justice" Dad whispered.

I laid Lucy back down, she looked somewhat peaceful. Miles walked back over and without saying a word, wrapped his arms around me. I could feel him fighting the urge to cry so I just held him, he needed the comfort.

"Clar, you should probably have a look through this" I heard dad say.

I looked and he was holding onto a notebook like the one that was in the other room. In his other hand, was a phone, an old flip phone. It must have been what she was calling me on. The phone was flat and broken but maybe the notebook would show any kind of evidence of what happened down here. I opened the first page and it read;

"The Clock Strikes One"

8

Day 1 The clock strikes one

I barely remember how I got here. One minute Harry and I were talking, having some drinks, and then I woke up here. I think he knows about the files I have. Of what happened to my sister.

He has dumped me in some horrible pit, there's 3 beds down here but only me. I don't know what will happen to me but I hope Clara finds him.

He brought me food but I had to do "special favors" in return.

I'm scared of what he would do if I said no.

The clock strikes one

The clock strikes one

Day 3

It has been a few days since he has come down with food, and I'm starting to feel sick and hungry.

I had a look around some of the other beds today. I found a phone.

I called Clara. I'm counting on her to find me. I know she will

Still no sign of Harry

Day 5

I'm so hungry. He came back yesterday but I didn't see him. I could hear him yelling in the other room that someone was getting too close. Maybe it's Clara.

I called her again. I heard him saying he needed to clean up the mess and find the files. By mess he means me.

I hope she remembers I need her to find him. Before Harry does.

The phone died. I no longer have communication with Clara.

This is the end.

SAVE
HIM

THE
CLOCK
STRIKES
ONE

My body was still in shock but now my mind was too. Who was he and why did I have to save him? Poor Lucy must have been so scared but I can't quite figure out why she's so adamant that the clock strikes one.

Then the memories came back and it hit me. I knew exactly what she meant now, something only her and I would ever understand.

9

It was the cabin all along, she was talking about the damn cabin. When we were kids and we would head out for the summer, the grandfather clock we have in there would always chime when it got to one o'clock. It was so strange and funny to us, we'd laugh about it for hours or make inside jokes only we would know, my parents would just shake their heads and laugh. I cant believe after all this time, that's what she meant but why is it so important?

I broke the silence, the room was still heavy with despair. ***"We need to go back to the cabin"***

"What? Why?" asked Miles, he almost sounded angry.

"Because I just think… I think Lucy wants me to go there and afterall, it's the one place I'm sure she'd want to lay to rest," I replied.

Miles's shoulders drooped and his head barely lifted to make eye contact with me but he gave a slow half nod and it was decided we needed to find a way out. I sniffled softly as dad helped me wrap Lucy's body in a blanket. It still didn't feel real.
Miles walked over to us and shoved me out of the way. Before I could say anything he was helping dad carry her body.
There was more path down a corridor to the left of the room that we decided to follow. We walked and walked and walked until we began to see light. Once reaching the end it brought us out right near the creek, the entrance blended in with the cliff face surrounding it.

"We can follow the stream, we know it leads into town, at least we can make our way to the cabin from there" I said as we walked through thick scrub and mud.

A few minutes later, Miles finally spoke ***"You have got to be kidding me"*** he exclaimed

"What?" my dad replied

"Look to your right, does the top of that DAMN shipping container look familiar?"

"Shit!" I muttered ***"at least we know where we are now, we can't just walk through his property, we will have to walk a bit further and cut across the tree lines. We know the cabin is near here so we just have to keep to the trees"*** I commanded

We walked and snuck and walked and snuck until we reached the cabin. It was just getting dark so we all agreed we would need to bury the body as soon as we could before the animals started to come out.

I walked off while Miles and dad dug a hole out the back of the cabin and laid her to rest. We hadn't gone inside yet, I felt so empty even thinking of going in without her. The house groaned under my feet as I walked up the patio's wooden stairs. I stopped, my hand resting on the door knob. I swear I heard something or someone cry. I sang out to the boys but got no response.

Distant cry

There it is again. What the hell.

I stepped down off the patio and walked around the back of the house, my phone torch lighting the way.

Dad had his arm around Miles and Miles had slumped into the side of my dad. I walked over and wrapped my arms around Miles. I could feel his tears soaking into the shoulder of my blazer as he got heavery, his cries got louder and his knees weaker. We sat on the ground for a bit, crying and holding each other. He was finally allowing himself to be vulnerable with me.

"Come on guys, let's go inside and get some rest. It's getting cold," dad said.

We made our way up to the patio, shivering and silent. The wood creaked under my dads heavy steps, as he opened the door. Then I heard it again, a soft muffled cry.

"That… Sounded like a.." i didn't get to finish my words before Miles interrupted

"Like a baby," he said.

"That's absolutely impossible. We haven't been here in months" Dad said

"We were only here yesterday. We didn't go in but we didn't hear anything either" I finally spoke

How could Miles and I have not heard it while we were here? That's basically impossible.

10

Dad slowly pushed the door forward, the air was still and we were all holding our breath. Not knowing what would be on the other side of the door, it slowly creaked open. We walked inside and Miles switched on the lights. A simple cardboard box sat in the center of the room. It was wet by water seeping through the roof. The box was still closed, but it now had a hole in it.

The crying had stopped but there were still grizzling sounds coming from within. I was frozen in the doorway as my dad rushed to start the fire and Miles made his way to the box. He pulled the top open and stopped. The crying started again, louder this time. I jerked myself back to reality and ran over. There, laying in the box, was a baby. A tiny baby boy. naked, covered in blood that wasn't his blood and feces that were his. He was trying to latch onto anything he could and he was starving. Miles and I never said a word as dad frantically paced back and forth trying to get the fire lit.

Miles picked the baby up and we headed over to the kitchen sink, filling it with warm water we began to clean him off. Miles kept staring at me, tears glistening in his eyes. I had been so caught up in this random baby, I had forgotten all about the grandfather clock.

"How is he doing Clar?" dad interrupted

I was still too stunned to speak.

"He's doing alright Mr Montrose. But he's hungry" Miles spoke for me

"We only have milk. I think there is a baby bottle the girls would play with in the toy box. I'll go check. It's not good for him but neither is starving" Dad replied as he walked towards the hallway, then he stopped and turned to face us again *"He would have to be Lucy's Clar. No one else has a key for here"*

I wiped away the tears now streaming down my face. I didn't want to believe he was Lucy's, she would tell me. I'm sure she would tell me. We had always told each other everything but I guess with me not being able to have kids, maybe she wouldn't tell me.
Dad had come back with the bottle and Miles started to feed the baby. He hadn't been fed for who knows for how long.

When the grandfather clock began to chime, I jumped, frightening the baby and causing him to cry once more. I was attempting to calm him down with Miles. It was 1:00 am when I looked at the clock.

"The clock strikes one" I softly mumbled

"Huh?" Asked Miles

"THE CLOCK STRIKES ONE" I said louder.

I ran over to the clock and opened it, Miles followed me with his usual puzzled expression.

"When Luce and I were younger we would open the clock, to pass secret notes. Once the clock struck one, one of us would go get the note." I flicked a little lever in the bottom corner of the big grandfather

clock and a secret compartment popped open at the base. I moved my head to the ground so I could see inside.

"There's something in here Miles"

My dad had now come over to join the commotion. I dove my hand in, pulling out the things inside.

A note.

A file filled with documents.

And a video tape.

"Dad, get the video player set up"

He went out to the hallway cupboard and brought the video player back in. The sick, sinking feeling came over me once again as the tv buzzed and went from static to the inside of an evidence room. Sitting in a chair was Harry, the other chair there was a girl, her face was still static. Then, her face finally cleared.

"Marley" I could hear the quiver in my dads voice as the words left his mouth

11

I could only see dad out of the corner of my eye but I could see his hand over his mouth, trembling at what we were seeing. A young Marley Jones, Lucy's sister. sat in an interview room, the time stamp reading 23:01. The most haunting part was the date. It was the day she died.
Harry was on the other side of the table and you could tell she was absolutely terrified of him.

~

"Does this place scare you Marley" Harry asked

"Yeeee...Yes." she shakenly replied

"Well if you tell anyone about what has happened, I will make sure you never leave here again"

~

You could hear her softly crying as she nodded her head, Harry started to un belt his pants and her cries got louder. I couldn't watch the rest. I couldn't let dad watch the rest.
We all sat in silence trying to comprehend what we had just watched. Dad had blamed himself for so long and we all believed it was the guy next door that killed her… but maybe we should've been looking closer than we thought.

Dads crackled voice broke the silence ***"How… how could he"***

"There's still more files, let's just have a look at them." Miles interrupted.

I opened up the yellow folder, staring back at us was the same notebook paper from down in the mineshaft. It was a letter for me, from Lucy.

My Dear Clara.

My best friend, my sister, my lifeline. If you've found this, he has already got to me.

Please keep my baby safe, I've called him Hugo. I know you and Miles will raise him right. I wish I could be there to help.

In these files, you'll find some things, disturbing things. Please don't feel like any of this is your fault, Clara. Because it's not. And it's not Jason's either.

Harry had been abusing me for a while, just like the others, but I got pregnant with Hugo. I told him I went out of town to get rid of the baby. That morning I found all this evidence. I stole it. Gave birth in the city and hid everything here. He knew I took it. but not where I hid it or about Hugo. Keep him safe. Save him

I love you all so much. I can't wait to see you again

Lucy xo

The other files provided all the proof of Harry kidnapping, assaulting and murdering 4 females. Marley was the first, then two girls from out of town and finally, Lucy. This man was a monster. There were maps and plans on where he buried and dumped bodies even different people he could make take the blame, including the guy charged with Marley's murder.

"He will rot in a cell for this Clara" My dad said as he placed his arm on my shoulder.

"I know, we can't let him think he has gotten away with this."

"But what if he has more of the town's police by his side?" Miles asked

"Shit, you're right. We have to take this to the city" Dad answered

Hugo started to shift and fuss in Miles's arms. I handed the files over to Dad for him to start packing them back away and took Hugo. Shushing and rocking him, with the addition of some vigorous butt pats, the grizzels lightened and he soothed back to sleep.

Miles stood beside us, ***"You're a natural it seems"*** he whispered.

The smirk on his face made me feel so warm inside for the first time in days. It was nice and I was so glad I had him by my side for all of this. After we packed away the files and agreed putting them back in the clock was the safest option for the time being. Still holding Hugo in my arms, I went over to sit beside Miles, who was now seated on the couch. I dozed off with Miles stroking my hair while I rested my head on his lap and Hugo nestled against my chest.
I woke to Hugo screaming, trying to latch onto anything he could. Poor guy really needed actual milk to fill him up, so I couldn't give him cow's milk again. The front door started to creek open, I shot up and dad appeared in the doorway.

"Sorry Clar, I didn't mean to startle you. I headed into the general store to get some formula and nappies for Hugo. No baby clothes though but I think your mum had a box of your old baby stuff in the attic. I'll check soon."

"Wha… what time is it?" i asked

"It's about 7am"

Hugo continued to cry. Now and then when he would unintentionally latch onto my armpit, he would stop. Miles was still asleep when I got up and started to give him a bottle. By this point, Miles was snoring.

While Hugo's bottle was cooling down, dad came back down from the attic with a tiny baby suit. I changed Hugo from the makeshift nappy made with pads to a real nappy made for him and dressed him in the suit. I had always wanted to be a mum. But not like this.
Hugo started to cry again, I had forgotten all about his bottle. His cries this time woke Miles. Half sleepy, Miles got up and went to get Hugo's bottle to bring it to us.

We agreed that we would feed Hugo, freshen up, head into the city and go to the main department. Harry needed to be stopped and we had all the evidence to do it. God, I hope we can trust them.

12

It's been a year now, Luce. We all miss you so much, I tell Hugo about you everyday. He looks just like you and we love him to bits. I ended up taking all those papers and the video to the city. Harry was arrested a few hours later, I even got to do it. It felt AMAZING! He is serving a life sentence. I really hope we got justice for you Lucy.
Miles and I moved with Hugo to the city, it's nice. There are so many more opportunities for Hugo here and I couldn't be in that town anymore, not without you. I try to visit you as often as I can and make sure you have fresh flowers. Dad moved back into the cabin so you're never alone, he loves being a grandpa and Hugo loves being around him.

****

I woke up to the laughter of Hugo and him crawling up the hallway with Miles behind him.

"Good Morning babe," Miles said as he stood up and kissed my forehead.

I got to sleep in on Sundays, but I enjoyed having my boys wake me up. Miles returned to the bedroom carrying a hot cup of coffee, and I sat up in my bed. Even though our relationship had only started six months ago, it felt like a lifetime. Or as Dad would say, soulmates.

bzz*bzz*bzz

My phone lit up wight a call from an unknown number

"Hello, Clara Montrose speaking, who is this?"

"He… Help… Me.. I'm handcuffed to a bed. Oh god he's going to kill me" the female began to cry uncontrollably

Miles was giving me a puzzled look, i can only imagine the panic on my face and just as i went to speak

beep*beep*beep

The line went dead.

ABOUT THE AUTHOR

Hello everyone, my name is Zoe and I'm from tiny Tasmania. I have always loved writing and found short stories to be my calling. I was getting too distracted from long novels and really wanted to create something for other people like me that love to read but just don't love the length. I loved writing this story and I hope that even just one person will love it too.